Imprint

Copyright © 2022 by homunculus books
Frenzel, Jacobi & Reinthaler OHG | Erlangen
HOMUNCULUS-VERLAG.DE

Texts by Anja Stiller & Alexander Rudow
Translation by Helen MacCormac
Some figures are based on characters by Arthur Conan Doyle (1859-1930).

Coverdesign and Illustrations:
Anja Fuchs, Nuremberg
www.anjafuchs.com

Printing and binding:
STOGA Print & Paper, Poland

Fonts used: Duality, Swagger, The Goldsmith Vintage.
Graphic material: freepik.com

All rights reserved, in particular the right to print excerpts and the right to photomechanical reproduction.

ISBN 978-3-946120-62-9

Cold Sophie

Holmes and I were enjoying afternoon tea and listening to a recording of the Christmas carol Adeste Fideles on the gramophone when the doorbell rang. A moment later, we heard Mrs Hudson's and Inspector Lestrade's voices in the hall. "Mr Holmes doesn't wish to be disturbed at tea time!"

"Let me through, I have no time for your airs and graces!" Lestrade shouted before he marched into the sitting room, visibly irate. "This note addressed to you was delivered to my office. Scotland Yard isn't your darned letter box I'll have you know, Holmes!" He waved an envelope in front of our noses. "I can't think how you put up with him, Watson!"

"Dr Watson, if you please," Holmes said as he took the envelope and opened the letter. "How very unfortunate," were his only words before he read it out aloud to us:

Dear Mr Holmes,

I am sending you this letter via the constabulary who, no doubt, will be greatly interested in your true nature as soon as they hear about it. As we both know, your great uncle on the paternal side was the notorious serial killer H.H. Holmes, making your interest in criminology simply the flip side of your criminal energy merely two sides of the same coin. To remind you of this, I have taken the liberty of abducting your niece, Sophie, who I might add is a very cold person, just like yourself - very fitting at this chilly time of year. As I am sure you will want to see your niece again, I have devised a series of puzzles for you to solve. The moment you fail, Sophie will die. Place an advertisement in the Times with your solutions and I will decide if and when to contact you again. For starters: How might one draw a square with three lines?

Sgd. Colonel Sebastian Moran

Cold Sophie Solution

"Cold Sophie," Holmes mused. "Poor girl, to be in the hands of such a villain. With Professor Moriarty jailed, Colonel Moran is probably the most dangerous man in London. And he is obviously out to avenge his boss, Moriarty."

"But what's this talk about a serial killer, Holmes?" Lestrade asked.

"Oh, I am afraid he is right about that. My great uncle Henry Howard Holmes made quite a name for himself in the United States. He was an infamous serial killer and fraudster. He confessed to 27 murders, declaring he had been possessed by the devil. A nasty story. Colonel Moran has journeyed all over the world. He'll have heard about him on his travels."

"But Holmes, aren't you in the least worried about your niece's predicament?" I asked.

"Worry won't help us here, Watson. Sophie is a formidable young woman and she is very capable of looking after herself, even in this situation."

"If you can't solve the question, she's done for, Holmes!" Lestrade cried. "So how the devil are we supposed to draw a square with just three lines?"

"Well, the way the question is posed gives us the answer. No one is asking us to construct a square using three lines. That would be impossible." Holmes took a piece of paper and drew a square with four strokes of his pen. "Instead, simply take a normal square and draw three random lines inside it. And hey presto, Moran's task is solved." He turned to the door. "Mrs Hudson, would you put me through to the Times advertising department, please?"

The Deathly Christmas Market

"Did you ever feel as if you were possessed by the devil like that great uncle of yours?" I asked Holmes as we headed towards the Christmas market looking for some light relief. "Don't be ridiculous, Watson. There is no such thing as the devil. We will have to rely on science and reason. Let's hope the next time we come here it will be with Sophie." The Christmas market at Tower Bridge looked truly enchanting. The fragrance of gingerbread and mulled wine filled the air. As usual, Holmes headed straight over to his favourite market stall, which sold marzipan and almond biscuits. "I find it fascinating to think the owner of this stall has a genetic defect that means he can't smell the delicious bitter almond aroma of his wares – even if he shares this unfortunate condition with half of the world's population. He doesn't even like his own biscuits or marzipan! He assures me that although he sells them every day, he never eats any!"

Even from a distance we could see a large number of people gathered at the stall, too many to all be waiting customers. As an experienced stick fighter, Holmes had no difficulty in forcing his way through the crowd with his cane without actually harming anyone. "He is dead, he's dead, he's dead!" we heard people shouting. Sure enough, we soon spotted the owner of the stall lying face down in a freshly stacked display of beautifully smelling cookies and marzipan. He had obviously been violently ill over his wares before passing out. I rushed over to him and pressed a finger against his jugular. "There is nothing we can do for him. Exitus."

"He must have had a stroke or a heart attack," one of the onlookers said. "Despite his healthy-looking rosy complexion."

"No, my good man," Holmes answered. "He has been killed by his own produce. He has been poisoned."

"But how can that be, if he never tastes his wares?"

The Deathly Christmas Market ## Solution

"Ladies and gentleman please move away from this stall immediately!" Holmes shouted. "Your lives are at risk!" The crowd backed away. We, too, moved to one side. Holmes pointed at the dead vendor. "His pink complexion is certainly not an indication of good health. In fact, it's a sign of poisoning by cyanide."

"Absolutely, Holmes!" I said. "Cyanide intoxication turns the skin bright red as breathing is disabled and the cells can no longer utilise the oxygen. As a result, the venous blood remains saturated with oxygen and appears reddish under the skin."

"Our friend has inhaled cyanide. The poison is fatal within a matter of minutes. Vomiting before death is another indication. He did not stand a chance, as he couldn't smell the telltale bitter almond smell. His genes were the final straw."

"But how did the cyanide get into his goods. And who is responsible?"

"The vendor had just arranged a new display of biscuits and marzipan. Someone laced them with cyanide, possibly using a syringe. By the time the poor man had unpacked his wares, it was already too late. There is only one person I know capable of such a perfidious crime: Colonel Moran! Knowing how much I enjoy the Christmas market at the Tower he wanted to demonstrate that he can murder people right in front of my nose."

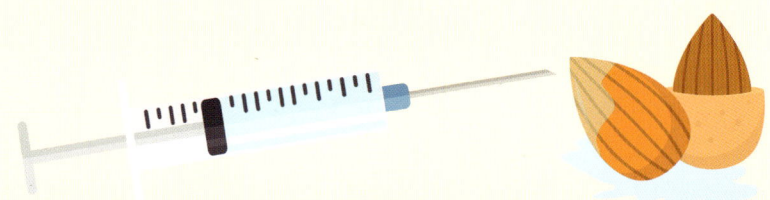

Detective Chess

3

Holmes and I were at home at **221B Baker Street** enjoying a game of chess. Outside, the first flakes of snow were dancing in the air. I was on the verge of a draw, or so I believed, when the door burst open and **Inspector Lestrade** marched into the sitting room. "The post has arrived," he exclaimed, slamming another envelope down onto the chess table so hard that the chess pieces flew in all directions. Standing at the door **Mrs Hudson** raised her hands in despair.

"Let's call it a draw, Watson, although your King would have suffered a smothered mate in four moves if our guest hadn't chosen to devastate the scene ... So, Scotland Yard has received another note for me, has it?" Holmes opened the envelope and read the letter out aloud:

My dear Holmes,

Congratulations on solving the first problem. You are always willing to let the press celebrate you as the brightest mind of London. However, by rights the title is mine. Therefore, I am sure you will not mind if I up the stakes a little. I devised the next problem myself. I call it Detective Chess. It is not about trying to checkmate the King, instead you must decide where to place the pieces. Draw a chessboard with 6x6 squares instead of the usual 8x8 squares. Set the following five pieces on b1, c1, f1, f3 and e5: King, Queen, Rook, Bishop and Knight. Set the pieces so that the squares can be reached as follows: 2 pieces can move to b2, none to f2 and f4, two pieces to f5, one piece each to c5 and a6. Once again, I will await your solution in the Times classifieds.

Sgd. Colonel Sebastian Moran

— P. S.: Your niece lacks any form of respect. It must run in the family.

Detective Chess   Solution

"What complete and utter nonsense," Lestrade huffed. "No one can make head or tail of this!"

"Oh no it's not, dear inspector," I said. "All we need to know is how the chess figures move. We'll have to draw a chess board with 6x6 squares."

"No need, Watson," Holmes said, dismissing my suggestion. "I have solved the problem in my head already."

"By my Auntie's bloomers!" Lestrade exclaimed, "How did you do it?"

"By staying calm for one thing. It is a question of logic. It says only one figure can reach square a6. That must be a Bishop standing on f1. If nothing can land on f2 and f4, the Knight must be on f3. That leaves us with the King, Queen and Rook. Neither the King nor Queen can be on e5, because they could both move to f4 from there, which is not allowed. Therefore, the Rook is on e5. For the same reason, the Queen cannot stand on c1 as she and the Rook would both threaten c5. Therefore, the Queen is on b1, leaving the King on c1."

After all these years, Holmes still manages to astound me.

"I wonder what the delinquent means by a lack of respect?" Lestrade asked no one in particular.

"Ah," said Holmes, "Sophie isn't a timid creature. She won't be giving Moran the satisfaction of having a terrified victim in his power."

"Good girl," I said.

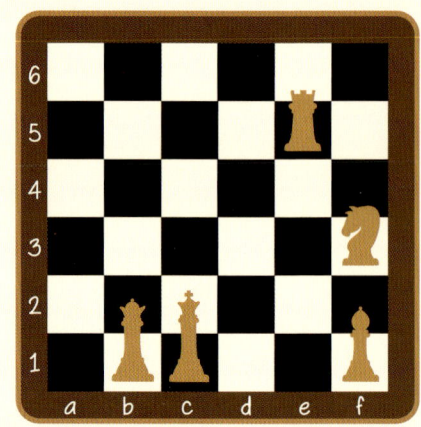

The Flying Santa

4

Holmes and I were out for a stroll in Hyde Park. It had been snowing and London was coated in a rare blanket of white. "I could really do with a day off from murder and crime, Holmes. See how Christ-massy everything is. It is delightfully peaceful."

"The unfortunate thing about a murder is someone always ends up dead," Holmes said, puffing away on his pipe. "But at least solving crime helps to keep the little grey cells busy, although I would agree that solving the Times crossword is more relaxing."

"The saying about the grey cells is a quote from your Belgian colleague Poirot, is it not?"

"Correct, Watson. But look, up ahead, what's going on?"

A crowd of people had formed at the edge of the park. We could hear children crying and saw parents pulling out their wallets and purses. Holmes hurried over with a few long strides. As I caught up with him, the cause of the commotion became apparent at once. Father Christmas was suspended in mid-air! He was hovering cross-legged about three feet above the ground, white beard, red hat and all, apparently sitting on nothing more than his neatly folded cloak. Below him was nothing but thin air and freshly trodden snow. He was holding a thin shepherd's crook in one hand, which rested on the ground, and using his free hand to point at the crowd. "You'd better placate Father Christmas or I'll punish you and your naughty children for all your wicked deeds!" he shouted. A considerable collection of coins already lay beneath him on the ground, enough to feed an orphanage full of hungry Oliver Twists. "Beware the might and anger of Old Saint Nick."

Holmes stepped forward. "If anyone should be worried, it's you, old boy. How about a night in jail? You are a fraud and charlatan and I've seen through that cheap trick of yours."

"What are you saying, mortal?"

The Flying Santa   Solution

Holmes started scraping away the snow beneath the flying Santa with his shoes. "For starters, we can't just ignore Sir Isaac Newton's law of gravitation, can we? You could at least have made the effort to smooth the snow over so it doesn't look quite so raked and stamped upon," he said as he uncovered a plate of metal.

"The power conveyed through the metal enables me to fly," Father Christmas said, desperately trying to rescue the situation.

"I suppose it does in a manner of speaking," Holmes said. "You could even say it is what your act is actually based on - your connection to the air, via the crook." He ran his cane up the staff, knocking its sides as he did so. "This crook is hollow," he said.

"Of course it is. That's how the power of the earth flows through me and allows me to fly."

"I don't think so, Father Christmas, Sir. There is a rod inside the crook that runs through your sleeve to a perch hidden below your folded cloak." Holmes traced the connection in the air with his cane. "From the crook, down your sleeve, then past your shoulder and down your torso. Then he tapped the Santa's folded cloak. It made a clanging metallic sound. "The fact is you are sitting on another metal plate."

As luck would have it, two constables appeared. "Officers, Mr Holmes has solved another case," I told them. "Would you mind handing over this cheat to Inspector Lestrade with our compliments?"

Theft at N°. Ten

5

Holmes raised his hat in greeting. "Good evening, Prime Minister." We were standing next to a decorated Christmas tree on the second floor of No 10 Downing Street. The prime minister's secretary, Mrs Parker, was standing behind him, sobbing quietly while Inspector Lestrade paced up and down, huffing indignantly. "The situation is very clear, Holmes, the diamond ring for the PM's wife has been stolen and the only person who could have taken it is Mrs Parker."

"Mr Holmes, you are my only hope," Mrs Parker sniffed. "I'm innocent. Can you help?"

The prime minister cleared his throat. "Indeed Holmes, we need your brains! It is my twentieth wedding anniversary tomorrow. To celebrate the occasion, I bought my wife a diamond ring. I was admiring it before lunch, and left it on my desk when I went out. The window was open but I do not think that is relevant. No one is going to scale the walls of No 10 during broad daylight! Even if anyone were capable of climbing the facade, the front door is always guarded and there are people out on the street at all hours. Therefore, the only way into my office is via the door. Mrs Parker ensures us she was sitting at reception the whole time. The police have searched her and her workplace and found nothing. She is such a treasure! I can't possibly imagine her sneaking into my office to take the ring..."

"Sir, I did no such thing, I beg you!"

Lestrade drew himself up to his full height. "Mr Holmes always says that when you have eliminated the impossible, whatever remains, however improbable, must be the truth. Breaking in through the window is impossible, as was sneaking past you at reception, Mrs Parker. Which means you must be the thief."

"Not so fast if you please, Lestrade," Holmes said. "I think you'll find that discounting the impossible leads to a completely different conclusion in this case."

Theft at N⁰. Ten   Solution

"Don't you want to search the office before you tell us what happened, Holmes?" Lestrade asked.

"It's not necessary. I have all the information I need. How did the ring disappear from the desk? We have already ruled out someone climbing in through the window or sneaking past reception."

"Well then, what did happen?" Lestrade asked, keeping a wary eye on Mrs Parker.

"Nothing was found when you searched the area and, as we all know, Scotland Yard is meticulous in these matters. Which means Mrs Parker must be innocent."

"Then we are left with no options at all, my dear Holmes," the prime minister said.

"So it would seem Prime Minister. We are looking for a thief who is not a thief."

"Are you trying to pull my leg, Holmes?" Lestrade asked.

"Most certainly not. As we all know, the prime minister loves a breath of fresh air, even in the midst of winter. And some birds, especially magpies, love shiny objects even if they are not edible. If they are suitably 'beakable', they'll steal them anyway and hide them."

"In their nest? Where?" the prime minister asked.

"Magpies don't take everything back to their nest. They hide things in different places, a bit like a squirrel in fact. I am afraid we won't be able to retrieve the ring, Sir. But at least you can keep Mrs Parker, who is a real treasure indeed."

A Kerosene Christmas

"We can't carry on like this," Inspector Lestrade complained. "I'm not your personal letterbox you know." We were standing in his office at Scotland Yard. Lestrade had called 221B Baker Street to inform us that the police had received another letter from Colonel Moran. "Our postal department opened the letter by mistake, Holmes. As these matters are of concern to the police, I read the contents. Let me tell you, this is one puzzle you won't manage to solve! I have looked at it from all angles. There is no possible solution. Moran is trying to lead you up the garden path. I am going to call in the special task force. They can turn the whole city upside down for all I care. We've got to find Sophie now."

"Not so fast, Lestrade. Let me take a look at the note before you send out the cavalry." Holmes said. He grabbed the letter and read:

My dear Holmes,

Here's a hint of the demise awaiting that awful niece of yours should you fail. Kerosene features in my plans as well as in the next challenge: "A married couple takes a weekend break in the country. It is late by the time they arrive at the cottage and it is already dark. The husband tries to light the oil lamp but discovers that there is only a small amount of fuel left. Not enough to soak the wick. "The kerosene is running out," he says to his wife. "We will have to sit in the dark until tomorrow. There is nothing we can do about it." – "Oh yes there is, my darling," she says. "We will have light in a jiffy." Sure enough, shortly afterwards the lamp is burning brightly." Is it possible Holmes? What do you say?

Sgd. Colonel Sebastian Moran

Lestrade grabbed the telephone. "It's impossible Holmes. I'm going to alert the special forces."

"Not so fast, Inspector," said Holmes. "All it takes is bit of science. The solution is in fact very simple."

A Kerosene Christmas   Solution

"How so?" Lestrade asked. "If the wick and the kerosene cannot meet, the lamp cannot be lit. Colonel Moran is toying with you again. Your niece is obviously getting on his nerves. So much so, he is looking for an excuse to torch her to death in the most painful manner. We have to stop this at all costs. I'm going to mobilise the whole Yard."

"Only if there is no possible alternative, Lestrade," I said. "Otherwise we will be putting the girl's life in danger."

"Right you are, Watson," Holmes agreed. "Though of course Sophie is not a little girl, she is a 23-year-old young lady. Her mother and grandmother were both suffragettes who fought for women's right to vote. Sophie has inherited their militant skills and an attitude strong enough to bring down the government. Things will be fairly uncomfortable for her kidnapper."

"I'm sorry to interrupt your little tête-à-tête, but the young lady's life is at risk!" Lestrade exclaimed. And the Times advertisement department closes in twenty minutes."

"Correct, Inspector. Let's be brief. We cannot lengthen the wick of the lamp. Therefore, the level of kerosene needs to rise. However, there is no more fuel. Luckily, we do not need any. Just pour in some water. As kerosene is lighter than water it floats on top. The wick can absorb the fuel once again and the couple are no longer left sitting in the dark."

The Magic Imp

7

Holmes and I had gone to the West End to watch the marvellous Pierre Palu's magic mentalist Christmas show. "Ah, I see the great detective and sceptic Mr Holmes is amongst us," Palu said. He was dressed as a Nisse, a Scandinavian impish creature with a full white beard and a pointy red hat. "I dare you to let me read your mind!" he said.

Holmes climbed onto the stage. "I'd be delighted, but I can assure you it is utterly impossible."

"Just wait and see, shall we?" Palu replied. He held up a copy of Charles Dickens' masterpiece 'David Copperfield' and handed it to Holmes. Think of a three-digit number where no two digits are the same. Now, write the number down on the black board over there. The board faced away from Palu, towards the audience, which meant the magician could not see the number Holmes wrote: 365. "Now reverse the number so the first digit becomes the last. Holmes wrote 563. And subtract the smaller number from the larger number." Holmes wrote 563 - 365 = 198. "Reverse the number again, please." Holmes wrote 891. "Now add up those last two numbers." Holmes wrote 198 + 891 = 1089. "Read out the first three digits."

"108," Holmes said.

"Go to the table and turn to page 108 of 'David Copperfield'. . Now, would you please tell me the last digit of your number?"

"It's number nine."

"On page 108 of 'David Copperfield' concentrate hard on the ninth word and then look at me." Palu stared into Holmes' eyes for a while. "The ninth word on page 108 is 'enough'," Palu declared with a triumphant smile.

"That's right," Holmes said. A murmur went through the audience. "Now tell me, Mr Holmes, did I read your mind or didn't I?"

"It's just logic and reason. Your mentalism is a simple trick."

Palu looked surprised. "You don't say?"

The Magic Imp Solution

Holmes went to the blackboard. "No matter what number I wrote down, the ninth word on page 108 was always the only possible answer. I'm sorry, I don't want to ruin your act ... but, let's say I had chosen the number 123 instead of 365. Turn it around and we get 321. If we subtract the smaller number, we end up with 198 again, like before. We can also turn it around again and add both numbers. The end result will always be 1089, no matter which numbers I start with."

"Well then let me tell you that it is no coincidence, that I picked you in the audience today. I found a letter in my dressing room, from an admirer or so it said on the envelope. He made it a matter of honour to challenge your wits today. It's only unfortunate that I had to sacrifice this trick to do so. The letter writer won't have wanted to miss the fun and is probably sitting in the audience as we speak."

"Moran!" Holmes exclaimed. He stared into the audience. "Watson!" he shouted, "There he is. Catch him if you can!" In the back row, an athletic-looking figure stood up and charged out of the theatre. He was gone long before I could leave my own row of seats. "Stay here, my friend", Holmes said, stopping me from taking part in a pointless chase. "Moran is not going to slip through our fingers in the end."

The Christmas Thief

"How charming to see you again, dear Mr Holmes," said Lady Dupont as she sipped her tea. We were sitting in her suite at the Savoy, enjoying the view across the Thames. Lady Dupont, who lived in Brighton, was visiting London and had invited us to join her for a cream tea with homemade scones, clotted cream and jam. Years ago, Holmes had solved the mystery of her murdered butler.

"The pleasure is all mine," he smiled.

"With you two here, I feel so much safer. There is a thief lurking within these exclusive walls! Would you believe it? A Christmas thief, I suppose. No one knows how he does it, but he has been breaking into one hotel room after the other. No one has even seen him yet. A phantom who strikes when least expected."

As usual, Holmes' interest was aroused, as the topic involved criminology. "Fascinating," he said, "A real Fantômas, by all accounts."

"As Mr Brecht would say: 'What is the burglary of a bank compared to the founding of a bank?'" I said randomly. Lady Dupont frowned: "It pains wealthy people like me to be robbed, too, you know."

"Of course, of course." I raised my hands to placate her. "Just a quote from the world of theat..."

There was a knock at the door. Before Lady Dupont could answer, a man walked into the room. He was about 30 years old, with pleasant features and a well-groomed appearance. When he saw us, he stopped and said, "Forgive me, Madam. I must have opened the wrong door. My room is next door to yours. I am awfully sorry." Then he retreated, closing the door behind him.

"What a charming young man," said Lady Dupont. "Oh, if I were a few years younger..."

Holmes asked, "Do you mind if I use your telephone?" He went over and dialed reception. "You will find the thief on the fourth floor. Young, slender, with brown hair, and he's wearing a red handkerchief in his breast pocket. Arrest him immediately and call the Yard."

The Christmas Thief Solution

The hotel detective held the young man in a firm grip. "Goodness, you'll break the poor man's arm if you aren't careful!" Lady Dupont called sharply. "There must be some mistake. I refuse to believe that such a charming young man should have anything untoward in mind."

"The whole concept of the gentleman thief is that no one believes they could do any wrong, Ma'am," Holmes explained.

"Surely that's not the only reason you asked me to detain this man, Sir?" the hotel detective asked.

"Of course not," Holmes answered. "Lady Dupont - I am sure you enjoyed the fact that this young man only had eyes for you. But how could he know it was your suite and not Watson's or mine?"

"I'm sure he addressed me first as a matter of courtesy, seeing as I was the only lady present," the Lady replied and smiled at the young man.

"Possibly", Holmes said. "But if he believed he was entering his own rooms - why knock?"

Lady Dupont could not answer that.

"Touché," said the hotel detective. "He didn't want to look like an obvious intruder in case someone was in the room."

Inspector Lestrade came running down the hall - "Scotland Yard has solved it!" he said, sounding somewhat out of breath. "This rogue specialises in older women. He makes a note of their room numbers when they check in."

"Older women indeed! Mind your tongue." Lady Dupont said, clearly sounding offended.

"Why don't we return to your rooms to enjoy some more tea and scones?" I suggested quickly as the young man was led away.

No Ophelia

Inspector Lestrade was in a much better mood. He seemed to have calmed down after threatening to call in the special forces. We were hanging up the Christmas decorations at 221B Baker Street when he walked in and handed Holmes the next envelope without any fuss at all.

"I'm as nosy as the next man to hear what Moran has written this time," he said as Holmes opened the letter and read it to us.

Dear Mr Holmes,

Can you sense the criminal blood pumping through your veins? Can you hear your great uncle applauding your criminal energy? Well, no matter. Let us move on to a treasure hunt. Where is Sophie? Let us narrow down the possibilities, shall we? She is not in San Francisco — but what does that mean? And she hasn't followed the call of the wild either. For the most part, she is an intolerable pain in the neck, ranting and raving all the time. I could do with a PO to keep her in check. I have reprimanded her 84 times but to no avail. Nevertheless, I digress yet brevity is the soul of wit. Kidnappers do not usually complain about their victims, but Sophie is no Ophelia. She is fair enough, but without a hint of obedience. In fact, she is the very opposite. Brusque and brazen ... That is no way to behave while you are under threat of death! Although it wouldn't be very original to execute your niece in this area. At least she can scream all she likes; no one will hear her here. Who knows, perhaps she will make it to San Francisco after all. I am sure you have guessed our location by now, Mr Holmes, have you not?

Sgd. Colonel Sebastian Moran

"Don't tell me you know what he's getting at, Holmes?" Lestrade said.

"Indeed, I do, Inspector! We haven't found Sophie yet, but we are getting closer."

No Ophelia Solution

"It's not that difficult," Holmes said. "Moran is letting us know that Sophie is still in London. The first clue is 'San Francisco'."

"I'm lost!" I said feeling slightly annoyed.

"San Francisco is a reference to London because of Jack London, of course! He was born there for one thing and we know he is referring to Jack London because of 'The Call of the Wild.' That's the title of his first novel. Moran is saying she is still somewhere in the city."

"And what about the rest of that waffle?" Lestrade asked.

"We can decode that just as easily," Holmes said. "PO refers to a prison officer here, but there is another meaning..."

"Or what about reprimanding her 84 times...?" Lestrade asked next.

"Which chemical element has the symbol 'Po' in Mendeleev's Periodic Table, Watson?"

"Polonium," I was beginning to see the light, "with the atomic number 84."

"But what has polonium got to do with anything?" asked Lestrade.

"Do you know your Shakespeare, Lestrade? Ophelia's father in Hamlet is Polonius. He's also the one who said, 'Brevity is the soul of wit'."

"Hamlet!" I cried. I know – the Tower Hamlets!"

"Precisely! The Tower of London is close by and people were executed there until not long ago. I think Sophie must be somewhere in the Docklands. She could certainly get a ship to San Francisco from there."

"The Docklands are vast, Holmes," I said.

"Absolutely! We will have to wait for further clues." said Holmes.

A Body in the Sauna   10

"The smell of pine needles creates a lovely festive atmosphere despite the circumstances," I said as we entered the sauna. "I doubt that's why Lestrade sent for us," Holmes replied and headed over to a group of three officers who were in the middle of a heated discussion.

"There you are," Lestrade called as soon as he saw us. "We've been waiting for you!" - "The inspector is at a loss as usual," I whispered in Holmes' ear.

"I heard that!" Lestrade huffed. "Well, you try your luck. Here's the body." The officers stepped aside to reveal a naked man in his mid-40s lying dead with a stab wound in his chest.

"Unfortunately, there is only one witness: the victim came to the sauna once a week with a friend. The friend testifies that they went outside to cool off separately as usual after the first sauna session. And didn't see each other during that time. The victim was stabbed to death in this deckchair. The outdoor area is large, with lots of bushes and trees for privacy. A 13-foot-high wall also surrounds it. You'd have to be a circus performer to get over that."

"And the two men were the only sauna users?" asked Holmes.

"Yes, apart from them only the owner was present, but he was on the phone to the building inspector in his office at the time in question. We've checked."

"So, where's the weapon?" I asked.

"There isn't one," said Lestrade. "We've searched the area with a fine-tooth comb and found nothing suspicious. The dead man had a book by Joseph Conrad with him and his friend an empty thermos flask. That's all."

"So, someone must have climbed over the wall after all," I concluded. "But surely someone would have seen him from the street...?"

"Not so fast, my dear Watson," said Holmes. "I suppose the man's friend denies everything?" - "Correct," said Lestrade.

"That won't save his skin!"

A Body in the Sauna   Solution

"As is so often the case, when everything else has been ruled out, we are left with the solution no matter how improbable."

"So, what does that mean this time?" the Inspector asked.

"The owner has a rock-solid alibi and you'd have to be a Ninja to breach the wall, and would have been spotted by passersby," Holmes said.

"We got that far already," Lestrade huffed.

"But you didn't make the right conclusion," said Holmes.

"It is impossible that his friend stabbed him, Holmes," Lestrade said. "Without a weapon? He hardly used Conrad's Lord Jim!"

"Of course not. The murder weapon was in the thermos flask."

"Now you're having me on! –"

"The only remaining possibility is that there was a sharp icicle in the thermos flask. The so-called friend stabbed his victim with it and then left the ice to melt. That is why we can't find a murder weapon."

Lestrade was genuinely astounded. "Sometimes I think Colonel Moran is right. It is your own criminal energy that allows you to think like a villain."

"My great uncle H. H. Holmes may have been a villain, but he was not an especially innovative one. His genes are little help in solving the puzzles of criminology. Those skills I have taught myself."

The Emperor's Denarius

11

"The Christmas season is rather jolly, don't you agree Watson?" We were ambling past the stalls in Covent Garden. Suddenly something up ahead caught Holmes's attention. He headed off in that direction. As we approached, I could see something glittering on one of the display counters. "Coins," Holmes exclaimed in delight. I knew what that meant. We would be spending the next hour or so occupied with coinage, alloys and marginal lettering. Holmes was a great fan of numismatics and owned a rather impressive collection of coins himself.

"You're an expert?" the dealer asked as Holmes pulled out the magnifying glass he always kept in his pocket and began to study the polished coins. "Well," my friend said modestly, "it's just a bit of a hobby really." However, the dealer had spotted his chance. Going by the number of coins in front of him on the counter, business hadn't been booming of late. "You'll find some genuine collector's items here. Like this one for example," he pointed to a copper-coloured coin, "it stems from the Thirty Years War. "Or this," he tipped an unimpressive-looking coin at the edge of his collection, "A Fugio-Cent..." - "...one of the first official coins in the United States of America," Holmes said, completing the dealer's sentence for him. He nodded, looking impressed. "A true professional. Wait a minute," he said, bending down to fetch a small casket from a box behind him. He opened it and showed them a silver coin on purple velvet. "A treasure for real connoisseurs. This denarius dates from the time of Emperor Diocletian. The mint date 46 BC is clearly visible. See?" - "Unbelievable!" we heard a woman next to us exclaim. Apparently, she had been standing beside us for some time, but we hadn't noticed her until now. "Unbelievable is the appropriate expression," Holmes agreed.

The Emperor's Denarius — Solution

"I wouldn't sell this invaluable unique specimen to anyone else," the coin dealer said, giving Holmes a conspiratorial look. "I want it to go to the right hands. Take a closer look." However, Holmes pocketed his magnifying glass instead. "I've seen enough already," he replied, "Thank you but no thank you. And you, my dear lady," Holmes continued, turning to the lady next to us who had been so impressed, "would be well advised to turn it down also. You would be purchasing play money, the kind children use to play shop." - "I . . . outrageous . . ." cried the merchant. "How dare you damage my reputation?" - "Be grateful, I don't call the police," replied Holmes. - "What's wrong with this coin?" the woman asked. "It looks very valuable." - "The most valuable thing about it is the velvet lining," Holmes explained. "The rest is fake. Great names, falsely thrown together. The Emperor Gaius Aurelius Valerius Diocletianus did not live in the first century BC, the era the coin is said to date from, but in the third century AD. At that time, the currency in use was the argenteus. Moreover, the date 46 BC makes no sense! No one back then knew that 46 years later a Saviour would be born or that we would still be celebrating his birth on Christmas Day, to this very day."

Foul Play in the Great Hall   12

"I simply don't understand," young Lord William said. He was sitting with his head in his hands in an armchair next to the bed where his brother Malvin lay dead. "He was right as rain yesterday. We spent the evening together and ate in the great hall…" – "You are repeating yourself, Sir. That's the fourth time you've told us the same thing," Inspector Lestrade said, interrupting him impatiently. He looked up at Holmes and me and shook his head indignantly. "This is no help at all. Lord Malvin is dead but there is no indication he died of anything other than natural causes."

I sniffed. There was an odd musty and mouldy smell in the room. My friend must have noticed it too because he bent over the dead man's face, wafting the air towards him with his hand. "You were in the Hall, you say," he said turning to Lord William who nodded. "Lydia had just brought us drinks."

"Lydia?" Holmes asked.

"Our cousin, she's gone to lie down. This is too much for her nerves." However, Holmes wasn't interested in the state of their relative's nerves.

"What drinks did she serve?"

"Whisky, of course. She had decorated the tumblers with sprigs of fir, with Christmas just around the corner. There were even little pine needles cut up and frozen in ice cubes. Lydia always takes such pains with everything."

Holmes nodded. "Tell me, Lord William, did you not have a whisky?"

"I certainly did. In fact, I drank mine first, before the ice cubes had time to melt. I prefer my whisky neat and didn't want it to get too diluted." My friend nodded. "Just one last question. When you and your brother are both dead, who is next in line to inherit your father's fortune?"

William looked at him in surprise. "Lydia. My father was very fond of her, too."

Foul Play in the Great Hall Solution

"What are you getting at, Holmes?" Lestrade's voice rang through the hall. He had obviously decided that he had been called for no reason and had sat down in a corner. "Lord Malvin died peacefully in his own bed. This isn't a case for the Yard."

Rather than answering the Inspector, my friend had another question for Lord William. "Did your brother's lips turn cherry red after he'd drunk his whisky by any chance?" The young man nodded. "And his pupils dilated, perhaps, and he turned pale?" Lord William nodded again. "He said he was feeling a bit poorly. He blamed his visit to the poor house two days ago where many of the inmates are ill. He thought he might have caught something."

Holmes shook his head, and then beckoned Lestrade who was still sitting on a chair in the corner looking increasingly bored. He asked him to bend over the dead man. "I smell decay already," Lestrade said crossly.

"Mildew," Holmes agreed. "The typical smell of taxine poisoning or yew poisoning, if you prefer to call a spade a spade."

"The decorations!" cried Lord William.

"That's right," said Holmes, "they weren't from a fir tree as you thought - but from a yew tree. It was yew needles in the ice cubes as well. Eating just a few is enough to cause fatal poisoning. However, by the time it got to that point, your brother was in his room."

"And I ..."

"... You are only alive because you drank the whisky before the ice had time to melt. If you had waited any longer, your caring cousin Lydia would be a rich heiress by now."

The Riddle of the Suffragette

13

It was already growing dark outside and temperatures had dropped significantly. At **221B Baker Street** a fire was burning in the hearth and dear **Mrs Hudson** had set the table for tea, with a plate of her famous almond biscuits. "I wouldn't mind a bit more of this sort of thing," I sighed but Holmes grinned. "If things were as quiet as this every day, we might as well . . ." He was interrupted by the doorbell. It was as if someone wanted to remind us there was no hope of peace and quiet for the likes of us. A moment later, **Lestrade's** voice could be heard down the hall. He sounded cross. "Afternoon tea?" We heard Lestrade snort as he approached the door. "Would you bring me a cup too please? And some biscuits!" He marched into the room, throwing another now familiar-looking letter onto the table. "It's a pleasure," he said as Holmes signaled to him to take a seat before he opened the letter.

That niece of yours, Sophie, is growing more intolerable by the day. Yesterday she insisted that women are at least as clever as men are, and as if that weren't enough, she then seemed to suggest they are in fact even more clever! Moreover, as if she is in league with the devil himself, she has set me a riddle, which is impossible to solve. She has gone too far this time. I don't care if she is the daughter of a suffragette — her pride will be her downfall. If your distinguished brains are as incapable of solving this riddle as mine are, she'll have caused her own death with her brassiness. Rope, poison, axe, firearm — all are ready and waiting. I just haven't made up my mind which one to use yet. Oh, I would gladly be rid of the bad-tempered shrew right away. However, I am a gentleman after all, so I'll give her a chance. Here is her riddle, it even rhymes:

Face to face, one side of me / illuminated for you to see / without that light I disappear / you cannot find me, though I'm still here.

Sgd. Colonel Sebastian Moran

The Riddle of the Suffragette Solution

"Ah, little Sophie," Holmes said as he put down the letter. "It's high time we freed you from the clutches of your uncouth captor. We'd like you to come for tea and entertain us with your clever mind."

"That's a lot of nonsense, Holmes," Lestrade scolded. "Your niece is putting her life in jeopardy and keeping the whole of Scotland Yard on its toes, yet all you can do is admire her brains. Face to face illumination. What's that all about anyway?" Lestrade crunched his way through two almond biscuits at once.

"I don't think Sophie should be provoking that dangerous man either," I said, voicing my fears that something would happen to her. "Especially as this problem really is impossible to solve."

But Holmes continued to sip his tea calmly. "Our Sophie is a romantic," he said. "Exactly the opposite of you two gentlemen, I might add," he said, smiling knowingly.

"Well, this is a fine moment for romance, Holmes!" Lestrade scoffed. "I for one don't want to end up fishing for bits of your niece in the Thames."

"What shines without any light of its own?" Holmes asked and looked at us both. "I'll tell you - it's the moon. If the sun didn't light it up, we wouldn't see it in the sky. Let's call the Times immediately. Sophie has gained more time to plague that kidnapper of hers."

The Fatal Audit

14

"An arms merchant shot dead, how tragically ironic," Holmes said. "And shot with his own pistol, a Walter PPK," the coroner added. "Two shots in the chest at less than 10 feet." We were in the office belonging to Simon Caralan, an arms merchant who was found lying dead under the Christmas tree in a pool of blood. "There is no evidence except for the fired gun. Not a single piece!" Lestrade complained crossly. "At least there are two witnesses waiting to be questioned outside. They are both in a terrible state and keep trying to calm each other." We stepped outside and found Florence Caralan, the widow and Julian Tavern, a leading employee hugging each other. "What a terrible tragedy!" Tavern cried. "There is an audit the day after tomorrow, that's why Mr Caralan and I were working late. And Mrs Caralan! She works in my office; she was helping with the paperwork."

"And when did you find the body?" Holmes wanted to know.

"I keep precise records of my working hours in this diary," Tavern said, ignoring Lestrade and handing the booklet to the famous detective instead. Feeling snubbed, the inspector cleared his throat crossly as Holmes read the last entry. "Your boss called you on an internal line at 8 pm?" he asked.

"Yes, he said I was to come to his office immediately. I dropped everything and went over at once. On the way, I heard two shots. Then I spotted a man wearing a black ski mask coming out of my boss's office. He got away." - "After that, did you touch anything or change anything at the crime scene?" Holmes asked.

"No, nothing! I didn't touch a thing."

"That's exactly what happened," the widow confirmed. "I came here as soon as I heard the shots." They hugged each other again.

"At least Mr Caralan won't be able to get in the way of your joint happiness any longer," Holmes said.

"How tasteless," the widow hissed, "My husband is not even cold yet."

"Planning and committing a murder together . . . that's what I'd call tasteless," Holmes said.

The Fatal Audit Solution

Lestrade put his hands on his hips. "Just because Mr Tavern and Mrs Caralan obviously know each rather well doesn't mean you can accuse them of murder, Holmes," he said. "As far as Scotland Yard is concerned, a suspected motive doesn't count as evidence."

"We aren't a couple!" the widow cried, trying to remove a lipstick mark on Tavern's collar with her handkerchief.

"Let's not worry about that," Holmes said. "I'm not accusing anyone of anything, I'm providing solid evidence."

"I'm all ears," Lestrade said.

"Mr Tavern, I was surprised to find that you had noted the call from your boss," Holmes said.

"I'm meticulous, I told you," he replied.

"Meticulous enough to record an entry after finding the corpse and stating that your boss had called you just minutes before when he was still alive?" - "Err yes, I mean no . . ."

"At 8 pm Mr Caralan is supposed to have called to say you were to come at once. And you said you dropped everything and went to his office straight away."

"Actually, I can explain," Mrs Caralan stammered.

"No, you can't," Holmes said coldly. "And neither of you can explain why the police couldn't find any bullet casings seeing as neither of you touched anything. Did the perpetrator leave the gun and pick up the bullet casings instead?" Mrs Caralan and Mr Tavern looked at Holmes in alarm. He continued unmoved. "And now, at last, we come to the motive. Not only was the murdered man a hindrance to your affair - so much for the romantic side of the crime - he also leaves a considerable fortune in the form of his arms business, and you know how to run it."

"All the way to the gallows," I said.

Hideous Mr Harris   15

"It is hideous," Holmes said, putting down the paper he was reading to look at me. "Mr James Harris. You know the man I mean, Watson?" – I nodded. "He's the head of the poor house, a despicable character."

"I totally agree," Holmes said, sounding angry for once. My friend pointed at the newspaper. "Not only does he force the children there to live in poverty, with no heating and barely enough to eat. Now the newspaper reports that he has been gambling away the funds of the poor house. Well, they are onto him now!" I nodded in agreement and was about to reply when the doorbell rang.

Half an hour later, we entered a warehouse down at the docks. An impatient Lestrade and two of his men were waiting for us. About fifteen feet above our heads, a man with a rope around his neck was dangling from the roof. He had been strangled to death. We recognized him at once. It was Mr Harris, the director of the poor house we had just read about in the newspaper. He was hanging very high up indeed. "Suicide?" Lestrade muttered. "But how did he get up there? Does that have anything to do with it?" he wondered, pointing at a small mound of ashes and a puddle of water on the ground directly beneath the body. "He certainly didn't fly up there and put the noose around his neck. And what was his motive anyway? Everyone knew he embezzled funds! It's never bothered him before."

"He didn't put an end to his own life," Holmes piped up for the first time. "His death is part of a very nasty scheme, and another message to me."

Hideous Mr Harris Solution

"How silly of me," Lestrade grimaced. "I should have guessed. Everything in this city revolves around the great master detective! Well, at least it wasn't an innocent victim this time. Perhaps one of the orphans from the poor house took revenge?"

"That could be a possible motive," Holmes agreed and Lestrade looked pleased at this unexpected praise. "But how...?"

"Look," Holmes pointed at the puddle of water on the ground. "These are the last remnants of a large block of ice, melted by," here he pointed at the ash, "a burning log, the remains of which we see here."

"So you think Mr Harris was standing on the block of ice?" I asked. Holmes nodded. "And as the ice melted..."

"...the support gave way and the murderer's work was finished for him."

Lestrade interrupted Holmes. "But Mr Harris could have arranged the ice block and the fire himself. Perhaps he had a guilty conscience after all?"

"Not at all. The murderer is no innocent orphan. I'm sure he's none other than Sebastian Moran, who has already told us that Sophie is being kept captive somewhere here in these docks. This just goes to prove how serious this abduction really is." The body had since been cut from the rope and was lying on the ground. Holmes bent down and removed a note from the dead man's coat pocket. He had been right. "Your truculent niece doesn't have much time left," he read out aloud.

Off with their Heads

16

"I hope you don't mind me opening your Christmas post, seeing as how it was addressed to the Yard?" Lestrade put another envelope on the table. Of course, it contained a new message from Colonel Moran. "This time you get to battle with a real super-brain, Mr Master Detective. Moran has sent you a riddle from Goethe himself without any comment at all." Holmes read the letter, which contained nothing more than a poem and the name of the poet, just as Lestrade had said.

A brother among brothers, / Just like all the others, / A required member of many members / In their father's huge kingdom, / And yet he is seen seldom / Almost like a child smuggled in; / They only accept him / Where there is no place for them

Lestrade picked up the hourglass on the chess table and turned it around. "I showed it to everyone at the Yard. No one was able to solve it. I bet you a pound you can't solve it before the hour is up and the sand trickles away!" he placed a pound note on the table in front of Holmes.

Holmes raised an eyebrow. "I'd rather not, Lestrade. Give the money to the carol singers outside instead. We'll have this solved in a jiffy."

"Holmes," I said. "The carol singers will be glad to receive a donation – but not even you can solve a riddle when the whole of Scotland Yard has failed to do so."

"My dear Watson, this time it's not just a matter of deduction; our knowledge of European literature will help us here, along with names such as Carlo Gozzi, Friedrich Schiller and Johann Wolfgang von Goethe."

"How come?" Lestrade wanted to know. "And who is this Cozzi person, anyway?"

"Gozzi, Lestrade, Gozzi," Holmes said. "He wrote a play called 'Turandot', which was later set to music by Puccini. Schiller adapted the play and the riddles the prince must solve to escape being beheaded – another possible clue to Sophie's fate, should I fail? Schiller's friend Goethe contributed a riddle for one of the performances. This is it, though the translation is rather shoddy."

Off with their Heads — Solution

"Right you are, Gozzi and Schiller," Lestrade said. "But who is the brother he keeps going on about?"

"You are too impatient, Inspector," Holmes said. "A poet has solved the riddle more eloquently than this detective can, but I'll do my best." He marched over to the bookshelf and pulled out a volume. "Turandot … Turandot … ah, here it is." He translated the title: "Produced in Weimar on the 2nd of February, 1802, based on the play of the same name by Carlo Gozzi and with a riddle by Johann Wolfgang Goethe." Holmes grinned at us. "It's in German of course. Schiller liked to change the riddles the princess asks Turandot from time to time. The audience greatly enjoyed trying to solve them."

"Well, what's the darned answer?" Lestrade shouted.

"You'll need a cool head to solve this riddle," Holmes said. "It was originally written by Goethe, who provided his poem for the performance on the 2nd of February, 1802."

"Go on," I said.

"Schiller penned the solution," Holmes explained, as he translated the words:

"The son who resembles his many 'brothers' / one like all the others / a member who must be smuggled in / a day like all the other days?" Holmes looked at us expectantly.

"Are we looking for a day on the calendar?" I asked.

"Yes, Watson! But which one?"

"Stop torturing us. Instead, contact the Times!" Lestrade demanded. "What is the solution, Holmes?"

"The answer is Leap Day!"

"One pound for the carol singers, it is," Lestrade said, looking at the hourglass.

The Clever Kidnapper

17

We had only just returned to 221B Baker Street when Mrs Hudson came running towards us in a terrible state. "Mr Holmes, we need your help immediately, it's serious. My niece's children . . ."

". . . Have disappeared," Holmes completed her sentence for her.

"How could you possibly know?"

"I can deduct it from your manner. We must go to see her immediately."

Mrs Linda Hagerty was waiting to meet us. She asked us in and showed us a small room with two neatly made beds. A copy of "Hercules: Myths and Legends" was lying on the table. "I came in to wake them this morning, Tom and Mary I mean, and they were gone. Have a look at this . . . oh it is so terrible." She held out a letter. The writing was slightly smudged, presumably because she had been crying. "I have kidnapped your children," Holmes read. "And if you fail to put fifty pennies in the box beside your shed, you won't ever see them again."

"And yesterday I was so cross with them because they had eaten a whole box of Christmas cookies. Oh dear . . . I . . . they are only eight years old, twins, you know."

"We will find them, don't you worry," Holmes said, trying to calm the desperate mother. "Could you show me the shed and the box?" he asked. Mrs Hagerty led us out to the little garden and we saw two sets of footprints in the snow. It had stopped snowing in the night, so they were clearly visible. Children had definitely past this way. However, the footprints were heading in the wrong direction, from the shed to the house instead of the other way round. "Have you got the ransom money with you?" my friend asked. I was surprised to see Holmes was smiling. "Without those fifty pennies they might not want to come out." Then he knocked on the wall of the shed. "Tom and Mary, you are two very clever children. But the game is up!"

The Clever Kidnapper Solution

We waited but nothing happened. "Why would they be in there?" Mrs Hudson asked. "Is the kidnapper there too?" Holmes, who was smiling away to himself, pointed at the footprints in front of us in the snow. Then he turned to me. "Can you see what I see, Watson?" he asked.

"I see small foot prints, but they are heading in the wrong direction, away from the shed."

"Just so!" Holmes really seemed to be enjoying himself. "As I said, they really are two very clever children and they know their myths and legends. He headed the few steps back to the house and then walked back to the shed backwards. His large footprints ran exactly parallel to the small ones. Mrs Hagerty gasped. "Those two . . .!" she began to say. "Don't scold them," Holmes insisted. "It is exactly what the cattle thief in a Hercules story does. He makes the animals walk backwards into a cave so that Hercules thinks they have been led away. Did you see the book in their room? Also, a ransom of fifty pennies isn't quite the sum a real kidnapper might demand, don't you agree?" At last, we could hear steps inside the shed. The door opened slowly and two children's faces peered out. "Out you come, the two of you," Mrs Hagerty called, too relieved to scold them. "Let's have some tea and biscuits."

Poison and Pills

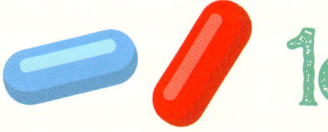

The Spaniards Inn was beautifully decorated with branches of holly and ivy, twigs of mistletoe and laurel wreaths. Inspector Lestrade was on his third pint of beer, drowning his sorrows. "This is enough to drive a sane man mad," he said, looking at Holmes and me glumly.

"But Inspector," I said, "at least you've managed to capture James Sotheby, London's most wanted killer."

"That may be true," he said. "But we still can't work out how he managed to poison those girls without harming himself." Lestrade downed his pint and ordered another one. "One of the victims reminded me of my own daughter," he sighed. "What an evil man."

I opened the Times and found the article reporting the recent events. "According to his confession, James Sotheby abducted eight young women and forced each of them to choose one of two pills which they then had to swallow with a glass of water, and Sotheby then took the pill that was left. It was like Russian roulette. One of the pills was harmless and the other one was full of deathly poison. And yet, although all eight victims died, fate allowed Sotheby to survive."

Lestrade took a large swig of ale. "That is what the fiend told us during questioning. But he must be lying. He is as cold as a cucumber. He does not believe in luck or fate and would never play a game of Russian roulette. How high can the probability of surviving be, I ask you . . . ?"

"Eight times 50% is 0.5 to the power of 8," Holmes answered. "Which means . . ." He did a quick calculation in his head. ". . . there's a probability of 0.4 that you'd choose the harmless pill each time. I can assure you Sotheby would never have taken such a risk."

The beer was starting to affect Lestrade's behavior. "You are such a smarty pants, Holmes! Why don't you tell us how he did it then?"

"All right, Inspector, seeing as the Times tells us everything we need to know."

POISON AND PILLS SOLUTION

A waiter arrived with a glass of Hebridean whisky Holmes had ordered a while ago. "Your double Scotch, Sir, sláinte and cheers," he said. Holmes held the tumbler under his nose and inhaled the peaty aromas. "Better late than never," he replied.

Lestrade hiccoughed. "If his Highness could get on with it, I would appreciate . . . those poor girls deserve a bit of justice."

Holmes took a sip of whisky. "Excellent! Now then, Inspector. . ." He took another sip.

"I can't stand this," Lestrade cried and banged the table with his fist.

Holmes gave him a withering look. "The short answer is both pills were harmless."

"Are you having me on?" Lestrade croaked.

"If both pills were harmless, then what killed the victims?" I asked.

"Read the article again, Watson," Holmes ordered. "What did Sotheby make those women do?"

I picked up the Times again and re-read the article. "They each had to select one of two pills and swallow it with a glass of water."

"There! You see?" Holmes said.

I began to grasp what he was getting at. "I get it! It didn't matter which pill the women chose because the water was poisoned."

"Precisely," Holmes said, eyeing his Scotch. "But why would anyone poison a drink when you can refine it instead?"

The inspector calmed down at last. "Now I can make sure that monster gets his come-uppance," he said.

Sophie, Sophie quite Contrary

19

Holmes opened the door, brushing the snow off his coat. "You can hardly see your hands before your eyes in that blizzard out there," he said. "Yes, this winter things are . . . ," that was all I could say before Mrs Hudson came running towards us. "Quick," she cried. "Quick, quick, Mr Lestrade has been waiting for half an hour. He is in the study. I'll take your coats." Holmes and I exchanged meaningful glances and went to find Lestrade, who greeted us with a grim look. "So, you have found your way home at last," he said. He was waving another letter in the air. "Thank you, Inspector," Holmes said. "Do sit down," he added pleasantly as he opened the letter.

You niece is becoming quite impossible. Dear Sophie has started ordering tea at five o'clock every day. If I don't comply, she plagues me with one of her lectures on women's rights. Imagine how relieved I feel that an end is in sight. This time you will fail, Holmes, I know it! There are three riddles this time and if I don't find the solutions in tomorrow's Times then it's goodbye Sophie, goodbye! Shall we begin? Riddle number one: If you do it you don't mention it, if you mention it, you don't do it. If you take it, you don't know it. If you know it, you won't take it. What could that be? Riddle number two: I have a head and four legs, but all you will see is a ball. If you touch me, you won't like it at all. Finally, riddle number three: You chase me and I chase you, yet neither of us can catch the other. Who might we be? Do not forget the answers; you will need them again in the future. Unless you fail of course. Then I will lace lovely Sophie's tea with a shot of poison tomorrow!

Sgd. Colonel Sebastian Moran

Sophie, Sophie quite Contrary ## Solution

I noticed the time on the grandfather clock and leapt to my feet. "The Times advert department closes in five minutes," I called out. Lestrade, who had ignored Holmes's invitation to sit down, started pacing up and down nervously. "These riddles are tricky, very tricky," he said. "Poor Sophie!"

"Don't worry, Inspector," Holmes replied. "I solved two of the riddles while I was reading them. And the last one isn't that difficult either."

"I wish I had your nerves," Lestrade sighed. For once, I agreed with him.

"Let's start with the first riddle," Holmes said, looking at Lestrade. "The answer is right up your street. It's false money. If you take it, you don't know it. If you know it, you won't take it." Lestrade nodded in admiration and I jotted the answer down on a piece of paper. "Now for the second riddle. A ball with four legs, we won't want to touch. What do you say, Watson? You might not be familiar with this creature but your veterinary colleagues most certainly are." I didn't have a clue what he was talking about. "A hedgehog, of course," my friend exclaimed. "Which leaves us with riddle number three: Two who chase each other but can never catch each other. In Greek mythology, you'll find them as gods racing their chariots through the heavens. Don't you know the answer?" He looked at Lestrade and me in expectation. "Come on Holmes! We've got one minute left to put that add in the classifieds!" the Inspector urged. "It's day and night." I jotted down the answer and dashed to the telephone.

A Shot in the Dark

20

"For Pete's sake!" Neville Stewart, director of the BBC, sighed. "First that accident with RositaSerrano and now the next calamity! Why couldn't Paulson do the decent thing and shoot himself at home?" We were in one of the broadcasting stations at Portland Place. Presenter Charles Paulson was as dead as a doornail with his head resting on the table next to a microphone, a magnetophone and a block of paper. A large bullet wound gaped in his head. He was holding a gun in his right hand and a pencil in his left one. "You seem more concerned about the radio programme than your colleagues," Lestrade noted, sounding suspicious.

"I was in a conference until a few moments ago, but it is suicide. That's quite clear."

"How do you know?"

"Quite simply because he said so himself," the director replied indignantly. "When his colleagues heard the shot and found Paulson, they switched on the magnetophone next to him and heard the following message."

He played the tape: "There's nothing worth living for any more. I give up. This is the end." Then a shot rang out.

"That's Paulson's voice," the director said. Holmes interjected, "What kind of problem was there with Rosita Serrano?"

"That was Davis's fault," the director said. "He was in the studio next door and put on Serrano's song 'Yours and Mine!' Unfortunately, he didn't realise the record was scratched. It got stuck while he was busy flirting with the secretary in her office. He even admits it. Therefore, we broadcast the same segment of the record again and again for minutes on end. The secretary had only just ended a liaison with Paulson by the way."

"So, the case is closed," Lestrade said. "A dead body, a suicide announcement on tape and a clear motive: Paulson was heartbroken because of the flighty lady in the secretaries' office."

"So it would seem," said Holmes, "but appearances can be deceptive. 'Yours and Mine!' is a long song and this was no suicide."

A Shot in the Dark Solution

"Are you saying there's been a murder at the BBC?" Director Stewart asked, sounding appalled.

"And I suppose you'll tell us who did it as well, eh Holmes?" Lestrade scoffed.

"Let's take a closer look, shall we Gentlemen? The first thing that should give us pause is the revolver held in the victim's right hand, while there is a pencil in his left one. I assume Paulson was left-handed?"

"I have no idea," Stuart answered. "Why does it matter?"

"If he was left-handed, he would hardly have shot himself with a gun held in his right hand."

"Perhaps he was double-handed, or maybe he was just fiddling with the pencil without using it," Lestrade mused.

"Just before he killed himself?" Holmes asked. "Anyway, there is more to come. When Paulson's colleagues turned on the magnetophone, they heard a recording of Paulson's message and the shot. So, how did Paulson rewind the tape after he'd shot himself?"

"Goodness! I never thought of that!" the director cried. "Thank goodness I've got an alibi!" he laughed nervously. "And Davis has too."

"I doubt his is watertight. How long is 'Yours and Mine!'?" Holmes asked.

"Nearly four minutes."

"Giving him enough time to leave the studio, flirt with the secretary to make sure he's got an alibi, and force Paulson to record the suicide message at gunpoint before shooting him and returning to his studio."

"If the record hadn't been scratched, no one would ever have suspected Davis," I said.

The Missing Wings

21

It was snowing heavily again. However, there was nothing for it but to head out into the cold. We needed to buy a few more Christmas presents and the best place for that was at the Christmas market. We were admiring some lovely porcelain candlesticks, when we heard someone screaming at the other end of the market, "Help! I've been robbed!" - "Watson," Holmes said, "I believe our assistance is required."

The screams had come from a small hut where a simple nativity scene was on display. The old woman who ran the stall collected donations from passersby who stopped to admire the wooden figures. If appearances were anything to go by, she needed every penny she could get. "Will you look at that?" she cried as we approached. "Do you see?" We did indeed. The Christmas angel's wings were missing. "Those beautiful golden wings, not real gold of course, but all shiny and bright! They attracted people to my stall. Who will want to come here now?" Holmes picked up the angel and turned it over. A sharp metal pin stuck out of the angel's back where the wings had been attached. "When did you notice the theft?" Holmes asked. "Only this minute, I took a step outside and when I came back, I saw a man with a dark hat and blue coat hurrying away."

"Well, he can't have gone far," I said.

Sure enough, only a few yards away amongst the crowd, we spotted a young man who fitted the old woman's description exactly. Holmes went up to him and asked him to empty his pockets. "Why should I?" the man asked. Nonetheless, he emptied his pockets for all to see without even taking off his thick woollen mittens. "Five minutes ago, I was buying hot chestnuts. I didn't steal anything."

"Oh yes you did!" Holmes insisted. "And now it's time to give back those angel's wings to that poor old woman."

The Missing Wings Solution

"How dare you accuse me of stealing? Who are you anyway?"

My friend politely introduced himself and then said, "Your loot isn't worth a penny, even if it seemed precious at first glance. It is not made of real gold. Yet those wings are very important to the woman who runs that nativity scene stall. It's how she attracts visitors to her little hut."

"I showed you – I've got nothing in my pockets," the young man replied.

"You did empty your pockets, true enough, but you didn't turn them inside out, which would've been difficult with those thick mittens on, anyway."

"It's freezing" the man explained.

"And taking them off would give you away," Holmes observed, adding, "Although it would give you the opportunity to show my good friend here," he pointed at me, "that injury you sustained when you pulled the wings off the metal pin. It's why you didn't wish to show us your hands, is it not?"

"It's better to be careful," I added. "If the wound gets infected, you can easily get blood poisoning."

The young man looked at us aghast and actually took off his gloves. There really was a small injury on his right hand, though nothing serious. "How did you know...?" he asked Holmes. Holmes smiled. "Well how did you know that the theft you claimed not to have committed had taken place five minutes ago? How about a deal? If you give the golden wings back to the old woman, we won't call the police. My friend here will take a look at your injury. He's a doctor. I don't think he'll need more than a plaster... but better safe than sorry."

A Prisoner in the Belfry

"A bit of stamina would do the trick," I said when we arrived at the entrance to Big Ben. "It's a 300-foot climb up to the belfry." - "Mens sana in corpore sano, Watson," Holmes said wryly. "After all those mince pies some physical exercise will do us good." - "Lestrade managed to get up there, after all," I sighed. Holmes had visibly fewer problems climbing the eleven flights of stairs to reach the top of the clock tower than I did. When we reached the steps, I was gasping for breath. "332, 333, 334 steps, done!" The Inspector was waiting for us in the belfry along with several officers from Scotland Yard. As we walked in, we saw a dead man lying on the floor. His face looked pain-stricken and his limbs were oddly distorted. "I don't believe it," I cried, "That's John Galt!" - "Who is John Galt?" Lestrade asked.

"He has been Professor Moriarty's cell mate now that he's been back behind bars," Holmes explained.

"He broke out of Pentonville Prison last night," one of the policemen informed us. "Rumour has it he was delivering a message from Moriarty to Colonel Moran."

Holmes and I exchanged glances. "If Moriaty learns Moran has Sophie in his power, things do not bode well for Sophie," Holmes said.

"I can find no indication of any cause of death," the coroner complained. "No wound, or broken bones, no signs of poisoning. It's a mystery."

"Carry on then. As long as we are up here, the bells of Big Ben won't chime, but obviously we haven't got all day." Turning to Holmes, Lestrade said "This morning, when the gatekeeper opened the door to the bell tower, which is not usually closed, he found John Galt lying there dead. What is an escaped convict doing in up here of all places? How far is it to the prison, I wonder?"

"The question we should be asking is, where was he trying to go?"

"Maybe he was waiting to hitch a lift with Santa on his flying sleigh," Lestrade joked.

A Prisoner in the Belfry Solution

"What's the first thing you would do once you'd escaped from prison?" Holmes asked.

"Hide of course," Lestrade muttered.

"The belfry is an ideal hiding place. No one ever comes here apart from the gatekeeper every morning. If we assume that the dead man was on his way to see Moran, and that Moran is somewhere in the docklands, then Big Ben is about half way there. I think it must be nearly five miles in either direction."

"That may be as it is, but it doesn't explain why he turned into a corpse when he got here," Lestrade said.

"John Galt hid in the belfry, but the door fell to behind him - which is why the gatekeeper had to open it this morning."

"Well, I don't think he died of starvation," the coroner laughed.

"No, Big Ben did the dirty work," Holmes said.

"The bell, you mean? How so?"

"In ancient China prisoners sentenced to death were often tortured with non-stop flute playing, drums and other instruments until they died. In European antiquity, too, the death penalty was sometimes carried out using loud drums. And in the Middle Ages victims were sometimes strapped to bells that drove them mad or killed them outright when they were rung," Holmes continued. Lestrade looked incredulous.

"You are right, Holmes," I confirmed. "A destroyed auditory apparatus isn't the cause of death. Rather, sound pressure causes the alveoli in the lungs to burst, and stress and panic finish off the job."

"It really is high time we found Sophie," said Holmes.

Justice in the Docks

23

We were enjoying our breakfast and I had just told Homes that I was very worried about Sophie's plight when, as if on cue, the doorbell rang. Minutes later Inspector Lestrade stomped into the room. "And so the farce continues," he said as he laid yet another letter on the table before grabbing a chair and sitting down unprompted. "Good morning, Inspector," Holmes said. He opened the letter and read it out.

I hope you remember the answers to the last three riddles! Alas, it will be little use to dear Sophie. If you do not manage to find the girl before Big Ben strikes 10 o'clock this morning, she will be taking her impertinence with her to the grave. That is what Moriarty wants and so do I. Assign a number to the starting letter of each solution. Then work out how the sum of those numbers can lead you to Sophie. I have already given you several clues as to her whereabouts. I'm afraid I won't be there to meet you and Dr Watson or that senseless sidekick of yours from the Yard, but I will be there, waiting in the wings, ready to carry out the sentence at 10 o'clock precisely. I will not say 'goodbye', Mr Holmes. Neither shall we meet nor will you find your niece alive. However, I am a good sport, so here are three final hints: Look for two numbers instead of one; you will find them by adding them; first the whole numbers, then the individual digits!

Sgd. Colonel Sebastian Moran

"We've got half an hour," Lestrade said. "That's all!" However, Holmes remained calm as could be. "Please fetch that note with the solutions of those riddles, Watson," he asked. I gave him the piece of paper. I'd written down the following words: false money, a hedgehog, day and night.

Justice in the Docks   Solution

Holmes looked at the first letters of the words - F, M, A, H, D, A, N - and noted down numbers next to them. Then he asked Lestrade how many docks there were. "Seven," he replied.

"And how many warehouses?"

"About thirty . . ." said Lestrade.

"Then we need to get to Dock 2, warehouse number 11." Holmes explained. He showed them the note. "If each letter is assigned the number of its position in the alphabet - 6 for F, 13 for M, 1 is for A, 8 for H, 4 for D, 1 for A, and 14 for N - and you then add them together, you get the answer 47. That is too high as there isn't a dock or a warehouse with that number. Therefore, we add up the 'individual digits' of the intermediate result, i.e. the 4 and the 7. That gives us the number 11. It's still too high to be a dock as there are only seven in all. Therefore, we have to keep going. 1 plus 1 is 2. The number of the dock! And 11 is a solution in its own right - it is the number of the warehouse - warehouse number 11."

We reached the docks a few minutes before ten o'clock. Even before we entered warehouse 11, we could hear Moran's voice inside: "For the last 2000 years women have had nothing to say in politics and it's worked very well indeed!" - "And so that's how things should stay for the rest of eternity?" we heard a female voice ring out loud and clear. The woman certainly sounded undaunted. "She's distracting him with more questions," Holmes whispered. "Clever girl." They heard Sophie once again. "I honestly don't see why . . ." - "To hell with you, you recalcitrant woman, do you never stop arguing? Enough is enough!" - "Precisely," said Lestrade, heading to the door with a gun in his hand. "Enough is enough!" By the time we caught up with him, Moran was already handcuffed. A young woman stepped out of the shadows. "There was no hurry, dear Uncle," she said sweetly to Holmes. "I think I'd have turned him into a true defender of women's rights by ten o'clock."

A Macabre Charade

24

"Thanks, but no thanks, I'd prefer a Cognac," Mycroft answered when Holmes asked if he would like a Scotch. We were in the Diogenes Club celebrating Christmas Eve. "I'll have a Cognac please," he ordered from the butler. It was snowing again; coals were glowing in the fire and the sound of 'God Rest Ye Merry Gentlemen' playing on the gramophone filled the air.

"So, who is the most dangerous man in London?" I asked. "Now that Moriarty and Moran are both in jail." - "They remain dangerous, even in jail," Holmes replied. "As John Galt proved, they know how to escape from jail for one thing." - "Which is precisely why they are being kept in different prisons," Mycroft added. "Moriarty remains in Pentonville, while Moran is in Brixton."

"I fear it is only a matter of time before they go back to their evil ways," I said. "At the very latest, when they are sentenced to death and see the noose before them, they will feel a strong urge to leave their current quarters." Holmes said nothing and sipped his Scotch.

"Well my dears, I have bought you a literary charade this Christmas Eve that suits the mood perfectly. It's a riddle by Theodor Körner, a German romanticist. Shall we begin our traditional Christmas charade?" Mycroft asked.

"Most certainly, my dear Mycroft," Holmes replied. "Let's see if German prose poses a challenge for those little grey cells."

"Well then, here is the riddle," Mycroft said pulling out a note:

My two together, / once caught with cunning,
through the weight of a third, / hang high on my first.

I did not have a clue but Holmes was already grinning. "And people think Germans don't have a sense of humour!" he said. Mycroft knew he had lost once again. He took a sip of Cognac. "Well, you might as well tell us the answer for the books."

A Macabre Charade — Solution

"It is a rather macabre riddle for Christmas Eve," Holmes said.

"I couldn't resist, when I heard about your success in capturing Colonel Moran, I chose it accordingly," Mycroft admitted.

"Gentlemen, may I remind you that I am still in the dark," I grumbled.

"Sorry, Watson," said Holmes. "We are looking for an answer in two parts, and it is hanging on part one thanks to the weight of a third party."

"Perhaps I've had one Scotch too many, but I have no idea what it could be," I said.

Holmes smiled. "The answer to this dark-humoured riddle by our German friend is the gallows rope. The rope hangs down from the gallows through the weight of the hanged man."

I groaned. "Gallows rope, macabre indeed!"

"Now, here's a present for you dear brother," Mycroft said. He brought out a longish packet from the cloakroom. "It is a new walking stick. It might come in handy during your next stick fight with Moriarty or Moran. Inside the wooden stick you will find an extractable blade."

"You are too kind Mycroft. Although our wits are the greatest weapon we have. Which is why I have chosen a game of 'Go' for you. While you, Watson, get an advent calendar with lots of riddles for you to solve next Christmas."

"Happy Christmas!" we said happily. "Happy Christmas one and all!"